THE USBORNE BOOK OF
SECRET CODES

Eileen O'Brien and Diana Riddell

Designed by Non Figg

Edited by Fiona Watt and Cheryl Evans
Illustrated by Mark Watkinson
Photographs by Howard Allman

Contents

Secret codes	2	Newspaper code	19
Letter swap code	4	Nifty number code	20
Pigpen code	6	Jumble code	21
Snail code	8	Dot code	22
Calendar code	10	Invisible writing	24
Telephone code	12	Double and triple bluffs	26
Morse code	14	Agent A's code kit	28
Code wheel	16	Code games	30
Technobabble	18	Answers	32

Secret codes

Codes allow you to send secret messages, anytime, anywhere. In this book there are lots of different ones for you to use. Some are simple, while others may take some time to learn. There are some coding and decoding tips on these pages to help you.

If you go through the pages of the book in order, you will be able to follow the story of 'The Tomb of the Cursed Tongues', which is introduced on the page opposite.

Use everyday things for your codes. Who would suspect that a newspaper could contain a hidden code? (see pages 18-19).

Tips for using codes

The person you send your message to is your contact and decoder. He must know which code you have used and how to change it back.

Never use real names when communicating with your contact. Use false names so that the enemy doesn't discover your true identity.

Choose a code that suits the situation that you are in. For example, if your contact can see or hear you, you could use morse code (pages 14-15).

You could type out your message so that your handwriting will not be recognized.

Disguise the paper to look like something else, like the dot code below (see pages 22-23).

Always destroy a message after you have decoded it. It may ruin your plans if your enemy gets his hands on your message.

Dear Mr. A. Gent,

Thank you for replying promptly to my letter. I will be only too h comply with your wis July 16th is still for your arrival. sure you and your will find 'Sea Vie remely charmir is a pleas ind Agents

The Tomb of the Cursed Tongues

A spy, code-named Agent A, is sent on a top secret mission to investigate rival Agent X's activities. Her quest takes her to an Egyptian tomb which has been discovered by Professor Felix, a famous archeologist. The tomb is cursed, however, and anyone who speaks inside it will have bad luck. Agent A knows nothing about the tomb or the professor until she begins her investigations.

By decoding all the messages in this book, you can follow Agent A as she uncovers the fiendish activities of X and his associates. Check your answers on page 32.

Codes in history
Royal code

At the trial of Mary Queen of Scots, lots of coded messages were produced as evidence. Mary claimed that they had all been planted in her apartment but, nevertheless, she was beheaded in 1587 for plotting to overthrow Queen Elizabeth I of England.

Codes in history
Butterfly signs

While working for the army, a military spy disguised himself as a butterfly collector. The patterns he drew of butterfly wings were, in fact, tiny plans of the enemy strategies.

Codes in history
Talking head

Over 2000 years ago a Greek spy was sent out with a coded message. The decoders could only read it when they shaved off the spy's hair. The message was tattooed on his head.

Letter swap code

In a substitution code, you swap letters of the alphabet for other letters, as shown below, or for symbols. If you like, you can make up your own symbols (see opposite).

Alphabet practice
Alphabet games are great practice for code breaking. With a friend, go through the alphabet, saying a letter each in turn. Now try saying it in reverse or saying every third or fourth letter.

Letter swap code

A B C D E F G H I J K L M N O P Q R S T U V W X Y Z

Continue here.   *Start here.*   *Go back to the beginning.*

S T U V W X Y Z A B C D E F G H I J K L M N O P Q R

1. For the simplest substitution code, write the alphabet. Choose a letter (not A). Put a line under it.

2. Write A under your chosen letter. Continue this alphabet directly under the first one so that the letters align.

3. When you reach Z in the top alphabet, go back to the top A and continue your lower alphabet from there.

SECRET CODE
KWUJWL UGVW

4. Write out your message. To write it in code, find each letter in the top row and swap it for the one under it.

To decode

Let the decoder know which letter you drew a line under so he can write the two alphabets. He can work from the lower to the upper alphabet changing back the letters.

These were the instructions Agent A received. Can you find out what she was to do?

XGDDGO
SYWFL P. ZW
ESQ TW
YGAFY XSJ.
LSCW QGMJ
HSKKHGJL.

This note came separately from the main one. It helped Agent A decode the message.

it Don't
too late in
ld
if it
rsday
. Please
know what
ns are as soon
u can. Thanks
again for all your
don't know what I

Keywords

To make a substitution code even safer, you can use a keyword. This is a word which helps you to sort out the order of all the letters in the code.

A keyword is between five and nine letters long. It must only have one of each letter in it. See how a basic keyword code works at the bottom of the page. Then use this method to decode the message below.

You can change your keyword as often as you like as long as you let the decoder know what it is.

QAO FNPQ RIMKOMX
BP MONYX. GOOQ GO
IH QAO EINQ.

*Agent X
sent this note to his
contact. Can you find the
keyword somewhere in the photograph,
write out the code and decode the message?*

*Agent X's contact
decided to create his own
symbol code, by
substituting symbols for
letters. Can you read the note?*

Keyword code

A B C D E F G H I J K L M N O P Q R S T U V W X Y Z

keyword   *The rest of the alphabet starts with B. A has already been used in Mozart.*

M O Z A R T B C D E F G H I J K L N P Q S U V W X Y

1. Write out the alphabet. Write the keyword (Mozart) under the first few letters.

2. Add the rest of the alphabet but leave out all the letters in your keyword.

3. Now use your alphabets as you would for the plain letter swap code on page 4.

5

Pigpen code

This code uses symbols for letters. Look on the page opposite to find out how Agent X used them to try to fool everyone.

1. Draw the grids and pattern of dots shown here in red. Copy the letters too.

2. Write your message. The pattern of lines, or of lines and dots, in the grid next to each letter is used to stand for that letter.

3. Under each letter of the message, draw the shape, or shape and dot, around the letter on the grid.

4. Write your pigpen message, using only the pattern of lines, or lines and dots, around each letter.

Start writing your alphabet at the top of each grid. The letters run from left to right.

Look at the pattern of lines, or lines and dots on each side of the letter.

READ ON TO FIND THE KEYWORD

Pigpen with a keyword

You can make your pigpen even more secure by using a keyword.

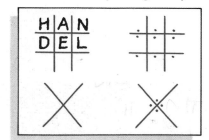

1. Draw out the four plain pigpen grids, with their dots, as above. Write your keyword (see page 5) in the first grid.

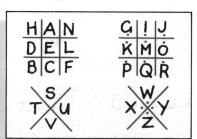

2. Now fill in the rest of the alphabet but leave out your keyword letters. Use the code as for plain pigpen.

Key tip

Make sure that your keyword doesn't fall into the wrong hands.

Always send your keyword separately from your message.

Better still, just give your decoder a clue to the keyword which he will easily find.

To decode

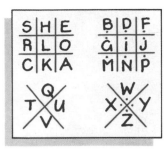

If a keyword has been used, write it in the first grid.

MEET ME

1. Draw out the blank pigpen grids, shown on the opposite page. Fill in the letters and dots in the spaces.

2. On the grid, look for the shapes and dots that are in your message. Write down the letter inside each shape.

Use the grids at the top of page 6 to solve this.

Agent X and his contact boarded a ship to Egypt, where X handed his contact a briefcase containing some ancient scrolls. He said, 'When we arrive in Egypt, take these to the tomb and remember which boat we came in'.

Disguised as one of the ship's porters, Agent A managed to get hold of the briefcase. She quickly picked the lock and found these scrolls inside.

To decode this scroll, you must find a keyword somewhere on this page.

SOPHIA

Agent A decoded the top message above. She didn't know the keyword for the lower message. If you can decode it, you will know more than Agent A does.

To find out what the scrolls were for and where they were going, she went to find Agent X's cabin.

Snail Code

In this code you use a keyword (see page 5) every time. See how to make and fill in a grid below. Make sure the decoder knows how, too.

Using the code

Once you've made your grid (see box left), here's how to code a message.

Making the grid

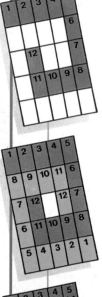

1. Draw a grid of five boxes by five boxes. Starting from the top left, write numbers 1-12 at the top of the boxes, as shown.

2. Starting in the bottom right box, write out the numbers 1-12 in the opposite direction. The middle box always stays blank.

3. Your keyword should be between 5 and 7 letters long. It should not contain the letter J. Write it in the grid from left to right.

4. Leaving out all the letters in your keyword, and the letter J, write in the rest of the alphabet in the correct order.

1. This example shows how to code the word 'Egypt'. Look at the box with E in it. Above E is the number 6.

The keyword here is 'pyramid'.

Remember to leave out J when filling in your grid.

2. Now look for another 6. It is in a box with N. So for E write N.

EGYPT

NKXZI

This is snail code for 'Egypt'.

3. G is below the number 12. The other 12 is above K. So for G write K, and so on.

User tips

TMUZ
IUMP

To code the letter j, pretend it is an i. The decoder will know that a funny word like *iump* must really be *jump*.

4. In the grid, the middle letter, H in this case, has no number. It stays the same in code.

PYRAMID

UNNI
UN VI
UTSETKHI

Send the decoder your coded message and keyword. He will fill in a grid, swap the letters and find the message.

Do keep some numbered grids in a secret place so you can send and decode messages quickly.

Don't use your real name as a keyword. Choose a false name instead. (See 'keywords', page 5).

Do keep the message and keyword separate, so no one else will be able to break the code.

I'VE SEEN THE SPHINX

Dear Marco Polo,

Release this piece to the newspapers to be printed July 17th:

QAVEEVRUX PCNUG
RAOWLCECGVZXZ KVUM
NUMVZOCILALM XCDQ
KVEELM HVXW VLHLEZ

Agent A found this note in Agent X's cabin. Can you find the keyword? Draw a grid, fill in the letters and find out what the newspaper report was going to say.

See the SPHINX at sunset

Now Agent A had a good idea about what was going on but she needed more proof. She decided to make her way to the ship's cargo hold.

Calendar code

This code uses days in a calendar month for the letters of your message. Most people have a calendar. Simply make sure that your decoder uses a calendar from the same year.

1. Write your message in number code (see below). Space out the numbers well.

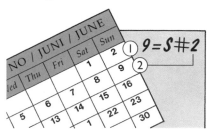

JUIN / GIUGNO / JUNI / JUNE						
Mon	Tue	Wed	Thu	Fri	Sat	Sun
					1	2
3	4	5	6	7	8	9
10	11	12	13	14	15	16
17	18	19	20	21	22	23
24	25	26	27	28	29	30

2. Turn a calendar to any month and find the first message number in the dates.

Number code grid

Write out the alphabet and number the letters in order from 1-26. Write out your message. Now swap every letter for its number.

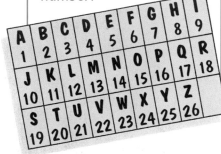

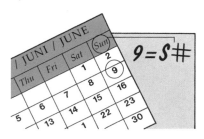

3. Look at which day of the week that date falls on. Write down that day's initial. Write T# for Thursday and S# for Sunday to avoid confusion with Tuesday (T) and Saturday (S).

4. If this is the first one of that day in the month, write 1 next to the initial. If it is the second, write 2, the third, write 3, and so on. Continue coding all the letters in this way.

Use the calendar on the page opposite to decode the labels. What did they tell Agent A about the gang's activities?

VORSICHT

FRAGILE

THIS SIDE UP

T3,W1,S1,W2   W3,T#3,S1,T#3,F3,W1
T#3,S3   S#1,W1   W3,S3,W2,T1

S1,F1,W1,
F2,T#3
M4

MANEGGIARE
CON CURA

BREEKBAAR

GEEN
LUCHTPOST

MANEGGIARE
CON CURA

ALTO!

To decode

1. Turn to the calendar month you have been told to use by your contact. Now look at each code letter and number of your message. For T#2, look at the second Thursday in that month.

2. Note the date of each code letter and number in your message. Swap each date for its letter on the number grid on the page opposite.

SOPHIA

JUIN / GIUGNO / JUNI / JUNE

Monday	Tuesday	Wednesday	Thursday	Friday	Saturday	Sunday
					①	②
③	④	⑤	⑥	⑦	⑧	⑨
⑩	⑪	⑫	⑬	⑭	⑮	⑯
⑰	⑱	⑲	⑳	㉑	㉒	㉓
㉔	㉕	㉖	㉗	㉘	㉙	㉚

T#1,S1,T2,W1
M2,W1,S#4,W1,W2,W3

T#1,S1,T2,W1
W3,T#3,S1,T#3,F3,W1
T#3,S3 F1,S3
T#3,S3 T#3,S3,T#2,S#1

This was the information that Agent A needed. She could now alert her headquarters.

Telephone code

You can speak to your contact on the telephone using this telephone code. It will sound like gibberish to anyone listening in but will make perfect sense to the trained ear.

Draw a grid like the one on the right. Fill in the letters and shade it as shown. Your decoder needs to make a grid just the same.

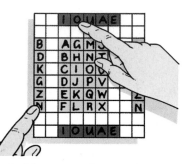

Ten boxes down

Nine boxes across

Coding your message

1. Write your plain message, leaving a space between each letter. Find the first letter on the green area of your grid. Put a finger on it.

2. Use your finger to trace along the grid from the message letter to a blue letter. Use another finger to trace up or down to a red letter.

Read out the 'words' on the telephone, pronouncing each one carefully.

'Ni ku nu' is pronounced 'nih koo noo'.

Leave a pause between words.

3. For each message letter, write the blue letter, followed by the red one. Each word of your message is made up of a pair of letters.

Decoding the telephone message

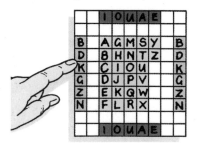

The two fingers meet at O.

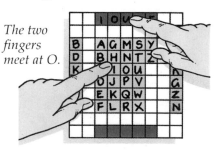

1. Write down the sounds as you hear them. Look for the first letter in a pair in the blue area on your grid. Put a finger on it.

2. Put another finger on the second letter in the pair in the red area. Trace your fingers along, and up or down, to the green grid area.

3. Write down the letter where your two fingers meet. Repeat for the other coded letters. Phone back your coded reply.

Having arrived safely in Egypt, this is what Agent A reported to headquarters. Can you understand it?
BINONO KUNI DADOZI GOZIZAZINOBA KODU DADOZI DAKUBUDI BINUZI NIBIZOZI!
This is what headquarters wanted to know.
DOBIGAZI BEKUKA BAZIZIDU DADOZI GUNUKUNIZIBABAKUNU?
Agent A's reply was suddenly cut short.
ZADOKU? KO GIKU DUKUDA...
Agent A was bundled into a van and driven to the tomb, where she was thrown into one of the chambers.

Morse code

Morse code was invented by Samuel B. Morse. It was first demonstrated in 1837 and soon became well known all over the world. Letters are made up of combinations of dots (short signals) and dashes (long signals). The alphabet is shown on the right. You can send morse messages in many ways, as shown below. It's a good idea to repeat your message a few times to make sure that your contact has understood.

A = •—   K = —•—   U = ••—
B = —•••   L = •—••   V = •••—
C = —•—•   M = ——   W = •——
D = —••   N = —•   X = —••—
E = •   O = ———   Y = —•——
F = ••—•   P = •——•   Z = ——••
G = ——•   Q = ——•—
H = ••••   R = •—•   End of sentence =
I = ••   S = •••   •—•—•—
J = •———   T = —   Question mark = ••——••

Tapping out a message

You can tap out a message on a hard surface, or on a wall between two rooms.

E = • =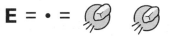

For a dot, make two quick taps.

T = — 🤜🤜🤜🤜

For a dash, make four quick taps.

• ① —

Between dots and dashes count one.

•••• ① ② ③ ••

Between letters, count to three. Count to five between words.

Always use these signals at the start and end of your message:

about to send •—•—
ready to receive •—
mistake or not •••••• understood

A flashlight method

With a flashlight you can send morse messages in the dark. The basic rule is count one for a dot and three for a dash.

For a dot, switch the flashlight on. Count to one. Then switch the flashlight off.

For a dash, switch the flashlight on. Leave it on for a count of three. Switch it off.

As for 'tapping out a message', count to one between dots and dashes. Between letters count to three, and between words count to five. Make sure that the flashlight is turned off while you are counting.

Bookworm Morse

It doesn't matter how many pages you turn at once.

Pretend to be looking through a book. Turn a page quickly for a dot, and slowly for a dash. Press along the spine of the book between dots and dashes. Study a page for a count of five between letters. Look up between words.

Later, a strange tapping brought Agent A to her senses. It seemed to be coming from another chamber in the tomb.

```
··
-·-/-·/--
·/ ···/·/ ·
·/···/·/-·-·/-·/·/·
/····/·          ··/·
-··-·/-·/-·/-·/·/·
-··-·/-·/-/-·/·/·
··/·/··/ ·-/·
```

```
-··/---
-·/---/-
··/·/---·/·/·/·-/·-
/····/·
-/---/--/-··
··/····
-··-·/···/·/-·/··/·/-··
```

Agent A recognized the tapping as a morse message. As it was repeated, she jotted it down and decoded it.

What did the message say and who sent it?

Thanks to the professor's instructions, Agent A escaped from her chamber and released the professor. As soon as she was safely out of the tomb, she set about catching Agent X red-handed.

Coding a message

Keyword has
cho
to

--··/·/·/-

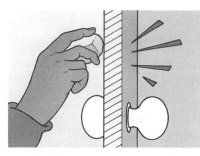

1. Write out your message. Now convert each message letter to morse, written as dots and dashes.

2. Choose a morse method that suits your situation, and send your message. Spell out each letter very clearly.

To decode

Watch, or listen to, the morse message carefully. Jot down the dots and dashes as you see or hear them. Then use the morse alphabet to decode your message.

Code wheel

Unless they can get their hands on this crafty code gadget, code breakers will remain truly in the dark about your plans when you use a wheel code.

You will need: thin paper; cardboard; glue; a paper clip; two pens of different shades; scissors; a pin; a paper fastener.

Making the wheel

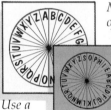

Use a different shade for each alphabet.

Mark the middle of both circles.

You could write a keyword (see page 5) on the small circle.

1. Trace the large and small circles from the code wheel in the photograph above onto thin paper. Write the alphabet as on the wheels.

2. Glue both circles onto cardboard and cut around them. Make a hole in the middle of each with a pin.

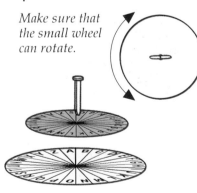

Make sure that the small wheel can rotate.

3. Push a paper fastener through the middle of the small wheel and then through the middle of the large wheel. Bend out the tabs.

On her way out of the tomb, Agent A saw boxes containing the real treasures to be sold by Agent X.

Find the key letter and decode the label on this box. It told Agent A where X was heading.

BCPBKDCT

This was Agent A's last chance to put a stop to Agent X's activities. She must act quickly.

16

Come to Captivating CAIRO

As soon as she was out of the tomb, Agent A promptly sent this postcard to headquarters, along with the note below.

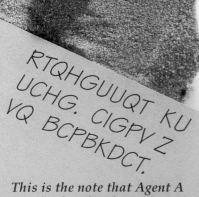

RTQHGUUQT KU UCHG. CIGPV Z VQ BCPBKDCT.

This is the note that Agent A sent back to headquarters. Can you decode it? Use the same key letter that you used to decode the label on the page opposite.

> The fate of Agent X was now in the hands of the authorities. All Agent A could do was wait.....

Coding your message

MEET ME TONIGHT

D is your key letter. *Use a paper clip to keep the wheel in position.*

Make sure that the lines are well spaced apart.
Code alphabet
Ordinary alphabet

1. Pick a letter, except A, on the small circle. This is your key letter. Rotate the small circle until this letter aligns with A on the large circle.

2. Write out your plain message. Find the first letter of your message on the large circle. Swap it for the letter next to it on the small circle.

MEET ME
PHHW PH
TONIGHT
WSQLJ
PHHW P
WSQLJ

3. Write this code letter under the first letter of your plain message. Code all the letters in your message. Now write out only your coded message.

Decoding your message

Make sure that your decoder knows your key letter.

1. To decode a message, first align A on the large circle of your code wheel with the key letter on the small circle. Add a paper clip to keep in position.

Key tip

For extra safety use a double-sided small circle. Write a false keyword on the side facing out. Write the correct keyword on the side facing down. If the wheel falls into the wrong hands, it is unlikely that the snooper will turn the small circle over.

PHHW PH
WSQLJKW

MEET ME
TONIGH

2. Now swap each letter of the coded message on the small inner circle for the letter directly outside it on the large circle.

Technobabble

In this code you make common words sound much more complicated. Work with your contact to build up a collection of code words. Start with just a few at a time and gradually build on your list.

CAR-PEOPLECARRIER
FLASHLIGHT-FLASHON
BOOK-PAGE TURNER

1. Make a list of things you often need to talk about. Beside each word write another way of describing it.

GET~TEG
PUT~TUP
UNDER~REDNU

2. Try saying other words back to front. Mix back to front words with techno words in your sentences.

For objects, think either what they are used for or how they work.

Try putting two or three words together to make one long word.

seat ~ bottomplonker
Wrigglewriter (pen)

Use the most unusual words you can think of.

Computer ~ Infogabble
Phone ~ Wirewarbler

Agent X's contact gave X these instructions in their last conversation.

(bus) Crowdcoach
★ ★ Maxitaxi ★
★ Multipeoplecarrier ★

You could make words sound like Latin, for example, you could call a cinema a viewarium.

Home ~ livearium
Bank ~ Stasharium
Cinema ~ Viewarium
Money ~ Payengive

For places, think what people do there.

School ~ learnarium
Gym ~ Sweatarium

> TEG ON THE MULTIPEOPLE CARRIER. I WILL TUP THE PAYENGIVE REDNU THE BOTTOMPLONKER.

It was interrupted by this message.

This was Agent X's reply.

> OOT ETAL! I KOOT ALL THE PAYENGIVE. IT IS WON IN MY STASHARIUM.

> NOT ANY LONGER, X. YOUR HIDEOUT IS SURROUNDED AND YOU ARE GOING STRAIGHT TO THE LOCKARIUM. I GUESS THAT TOMB HAD A CURSE ON IT AFTER ALL.

Newspaper code

Marking a message

A newspaper can be very useful for sending a secret message. You won't have to look far to find one and no one is likely to wonder what you are doing with it.

Can you read the message that headquarters sent to Agent A when this article appeared in the newspapers?

This hole tells the decoder which page to look on.

SATURDAY, JANUARY 18TH

it was lucky the professor
new morse code and
s able to tap o

1. Choose any number in the date on the front of a newspaper. Pierce above this number with a pin.

> It was at this time that th
> many times during the f
> when it became apparen

Pierce your message letters in order down the page.

2. Open the newspaper at this page number. Use the pin to prick holes above the printed letters which spell your message words.

> It was at this time that th
> many times during the f
> when it became apparen
> for **SAME TIME**

3. At the end of a word put a hole in the next space between words. This will help your decoder to read swiftly.

To decode

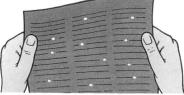

The decoder will hold the message page up to the light. He will see the holes and read your message.

SATURDAY, JANUARY 18TH

Professor locked in tomb for four weeks!

Professor Felix, an archeologist, finally discovered the tomb he has spent a lifetime looking for, only to be made a prisoner there for four weeks.

"The Tomb of the Cursed Tongues" is mentioned in ancient scripts but until now no one knew where it was. The professor had only just stumbled upon the tomb when two crooks, who had been following him, kidnapped him. The professor said,

Professor Felix, pictured here minutes after escaping his four week ordeal.

"I had to watch as, over the weeks, they took away every piece of treasure. They then replaced the treasure with forgeries. Luckily I knew not to speak. The crooks talked a lot in the tomb. I think the curse must have worked."

The professor and an agent, also held, escaped through a secret exit.

Nifty number code

A B C D E F G H I J K L M N O P Q R S T U V W X Y Z
① ② ③ ④ ⑤

1. Write the letters of the alphabet in a row. Number each vowel 1-5, in order.

2. Look for your first message letter in the alphabet. In this example it is M.

3. Look for the vowel to the left of the message letter. In this example it is I.

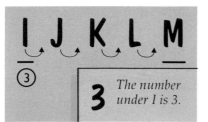

③ **3** *The number under I is 3.*

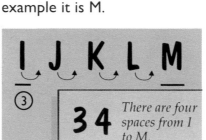

③ **34** *There are four spaces from I to M.*

Put a dot between letters.

34.2.2 45

4. Write the number that is under the vowel. Count the spaces between the vowel and your message letter.

5. Write the number of spaces after the vowel number. This pair of numbers is the code for the first letter.

6. Repeat this for all of your message letters. For a vowel, just write down the single number that is under it.

Here are the names of some Egyptian treasures found in the tomb. Can you decode them?

To decode

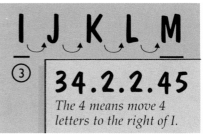

③ **34.2.2.45**
The 4 means move 4 letters to the right of I.

For number pairs, find the vowel above the first number in a pair. The second number tells you how many letters you should count to the right of that vowel to find your letter.

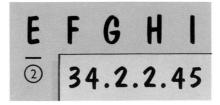

E F G H I
② **34.2.2.45**

For single numbers, look for the vowel above that number. Write down that vowel.

44.41.23. 3.35. 53

23.2.1.13. 13.43.2.44.44

11.2.1. 13.44

34.5.34. 34.54

ORSICHT
FRAGILE
FRÁGIL
FRAGILE

Jumble code

This code works because red tissue paper lets some pen shades show through, but not others. You can give your decoder a jumble of letters or pictures, but through tissue paper he will see a clear message.

You will need: red tissue paper (available from most art stores); pens of different shades; pale paper.

You could use red cellophane instead of tissue paper.

1. Write your message with a purple, green, black or blue pen. Put big gaps between the letters. Use the whole page.

2. In between and on top of your message letters, write a false message, or just lots of letters, with a red pen.

Lay some red tissue paper over this confusing map to reveal the real map that led Professor Felix to 'The Tomb of the Cursed Tongues'.

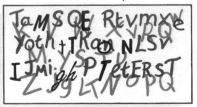

3. Choose an orange or yellow pen and write a second bluff message, or lots of letters, in the same way.

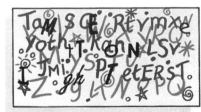

4. Now add some small pictures or dots to use up any leftover space and to make it more confusing.

To decode

Lay some red tissue paper over the message. The red, yellow and orange letters will disappear, leaving only the message written with a dark pen.

Dot code

With a little sneaky doodling and a simple code strip, you can disguise your message as a picture, or to confuse your code-breaker even further, as an important-looking chart.

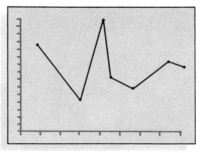

JULY 4 TO JULY 10

Look at the peaks of the graph on this picture.

The graph, the picture and the map on these two pages are actually dot codes. Make a strip with 0.5cm (¼in) marks (see below) to find out three cities where Agent X sold treasures from the tomb.

Making a code strip

Start from the left edge of the paper.

1. Use a piece of paper at least 13cm (5in) wide. With a ruler, make a mark along the edge every 0.5cm (¼in).

A B C D E

2. Write A between the left edge of the paper and the first mark. Add the rest of the alphabet in the spaces.

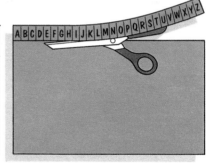

ABCDEFGHIJKLMNOPQRSTUVWXYZ

3. Draw a line under your alphabet and cut out the strip. Your decoder will need to make an identical strip.

Making a picture dot message

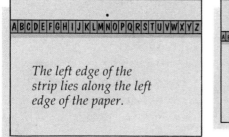

ABCDEFGHIJKLMNOPQRSTUVWXYZ

The left edge of the strip lies along the left edge of the paper.

1. Hold your strip near the top of a piece of paper. Draw a dot over the first letter in your message.

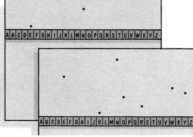

2. Move the strip down a little. Put a dot over the second message letter. Finish your message like this.

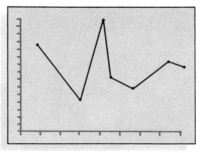

3. You could disguise your dot pattern as a picture or a graph, like the one shown in the picture above.

Look carefully at the 'Burial sites' on this map.

Note the stars in this picture.

You might find it easier to hold the strip if you leave extra space on each end.

KEY:
BURIAL SITES
10 MIN. WALK

A B C D E F G H I J K L M N O P Q R

To decode

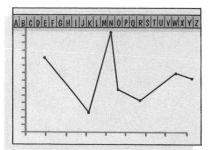

1. Lay your strip along the top of the paper, with the left edge of the strip lying along the left edge of the paper.

Keep the strip straight as you slowly move it down the paper.

Read through the letters and find the words and message.

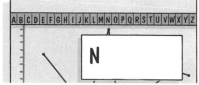

N

2. Move the strip down the paper. When the top edge of the strip meets a dot, make a note of the letter under it.

Tips

You can make bigger drawings by using a code strip with 1cm (½in) markings.

Make sure both coding and decoding strips have the same measurements.

23

Invisible writing

Here are some ways to send short, top secret messages that are completely invisible until they are revealed by those cunning enough to know how.

Invisible inks

You can write invisible messages using everyday things. Find out below how to make the inks visible again.

You can write an invisible message with any of these ingredients.

Potato juice

Lemon juice

Candle wax

Juicy message

As the juice dries, the message becomes invisible.

To make invisible ink, either grate a raw potato and squeeze the gratings over a saucer, or squeeze half a lemon. Dip a cotton-tipped stick, or a toothpick, into the juice and write your message on pale paper.

Wax message

Cut the wick from the top of a white candle. Write your message using the candle as a pen. Use pale paper. Press hard while writing your message. Brush off any loose wax when you have finished writing your message.

Making your message visible

You might need to rub the powder into the wax a little.

For lemon and potato messages, heat your oven to 120°C, 250°F, Gas Mark 2. Place the paper on the top shelf for 5-10 minutes, or until the juice has turned brown.

For wax, sprinkle the paper with coffee powder, chalk dust (use dark chalk) or fine soil. Then shake it off very gently. The grains will stick only to the wax message.

Giving a clue

If you are going to write an invisible message, you will need to let your decoder know where to find it. On this page, you will find some good ways to do this.

Decide with your decoder on an initial code to show what kind of invisible message is inside. For instance, L is for lemon, P is for potato and C is for candle wax.

The day can be used to show where exactly the message is. For instance:

Monday = along the sides
Tuesday = between lines
Wednesday = on the back

Potato message inside

Potato message written along the sides

Alexander C. Crets
Woodview
Bond Street
SPY 007

The letter C shows that there is a wax message inside.

Dear Alexander

Diabolo
Mauna Kea

Tuesday, May 2nd

Hope you're feeling better after your very unpleasant encounter with next door's chimpanzee.

I still can't imagine how it got into your house. You must have been devastated that your entire collection of false teeth had been completely ruined.

Yours
Ann Non

Message will show up between the lines

This message tells you the code names of two of Agent A's contacts.

The message is made visible with coffee powder.

Lemon message inside

S. P. O'Nage
1 Mission Way
Agentsville

L. E. Mentry
38 Shady Lane
Hideaway

Both of these messages tell you the names of some of Agent X's contacts.

Wig Wam

Monday, August 22nd

Dear Miss O'Nage

Congratulations!
You have been chosen from a large number of applicants to represent Agentsville in the national pie-eating final. The big event will be held on July 4th of next year. Please contact Mr. Bloo Berry of the Pie-eaters Association as soon as possible.

Yours,
Mr. Indy Gestion
Chairman of the Pie-eaters Association

Monday, January 28th

Dear Lisa

Thank you for your letter enquiring about our fabulous 'Get to know your walrus' weekends on offer this Summer. Our trained staff and expert animal psychologists will be on hand and we are always willing to answer any questions you might have. You will find one of our brochures enclosed, along with a price list.

Yours,
Hugh Tusks

The message is along the side of the letter.

Double and triple bluffs

A clever agent may bluff, or fool any spies by sending a double- or triple-coded message. This means using two or three codes on the same message to make it extra safe. Make sure that your decoder knows any key words or letters needed to crack the codes.

Coding a message

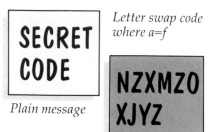

SECRET CODE

Letter swap code where a=f

Plain message

NZXMZO XJYZ

1. First write out your message. Then write it in one code.

NZXMZO XJYZ

EPYUPC YTXP

Letter swap message written in snail code, keyword 'pyramid'

2. Now write this coded message in a second code.

EPYUPC YTXP

You can only use symbols for the last encoding.

Snail code message written in pigpen

3. For triple bluffs, code the message for a third time.

Safe bluffs

For extra safety, devise a set of symbols to represent each type of code and keyword. These should be known only by the coder and decoder.

Letter swap code......
(a = g)
Pages 4-5
Pigpen code...............
Pages 6-7
Snail code...................
Pages 8-9
Calendar code...........
Pages 10-11
Telephone code.........
Pages 12-13
Morse code.................
Pages 14-15
Code wheel.................
(a = d)
Pages 16-17

Technobabble.............
Page 18
Nifty Number code..
Page 20
Jumble code................
Page 21
Dot code.......................
Pages 22-23
Invisible writing..........
Pages 24-25

Keywords:
For a keyword symbol, choose something that is associated with the keyword. Here are some examples.

Handel (musician)...
Dickens (writer)......
Sophie.......................

Double bluffs

To decode the following three messages, first decode using the code shown by the first symbol given. Then decode that new message with the code shown by the second symbol in each case.

The following three messages tell how the 'Tomb of the Cursed Tongues' got its name. They were written by King Tutnam, an ancient Egyptian pharoah and secret code expert.

Follow the code symbols from left to right.

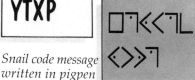

Triple bluffs

Try decoding the messages below by using the first code given, then the second, then the third.

The story continues with this message.

32.4
    13.4.11.3.22.1.55.3
35.4.32.5.32.3.55.4.55.3.22.3
13.4.32.4.11.5   32.4.13.5
11.3   13.1.32.5.11.5.13.3
32.5.13.5.
55.1.13.4.32.4.32.3.13.4
13.4.11.3.22.1.55.3   32.4
22.5.35.4.11.3.32.3.55.3.22.3
11.3   32.3.32.1.35.5.11.1.55.3

☺ ◎

These messages are all clues to an object which is very useful when using codes. Can you decode the clues? Do you know what the object is?

54.44.45 51.5.55
43.31.3.43.21.45
53.11.12.51.45
42.51.41.11.23.51 54.44.45
45.44.43.23.44

Letter swap code using the keyword 'Handel'

☺ ♪ ◎

KNBZNO DFZ MYOKPM RN
LFO LZAJ MFKEE FKXO JKS
EGQP FO QKNNZL MYOKP
IZT LFO TOML ZI FRM ERIO.

If your code uses a keyword, try to combine both symbols. This is snail code with the keyword 'Dickens'.

◎ ◎

The code and keyword symbols have been combined here. Can you tell what they are? 🐷 🌸ₛ ⓜ 💬

TXMJ TXKJ
WRTJWXWX TDWR
IJTDWDPRKJ MRTJMJ
TXMJ TRKRMDMDTDMJ
KJPDIRKRIX

◎ⓠ ↻ₕ ◎

Agent A's code kit

You can keep all you need for emergency coding in a tiny box. Agent A disguised hers as a sewing kit and kept it in her pocket.

This is the actual size of Agent A's code kit. Everything she needed fitted inside, as shown here.

Tape for wrapping a winding code (see below) around a pencil. Use a short pencil that fits inside the box.

SEWING KIT

Piece of candle wax for invisible writing (pages 24-25)

Spare winding code strips (see the opposite page)

Squash a code snake (see the opposite page) into a small cube and tie it with thread.

Blank snail code grids (pages 8-9)

Fold up a telephone code card (pages 12-13) so that it fits inside the box.

Winding code

You can write lines under each other all around the pencil.

Make sure that your decoder has a pencil of the same thickness.

1. Cut a strip of paper 1cm (½in) wide. Tape it at a slant near one end of a pencil, as shown above.

2. Wrap the paper around the pencil so that the coils lie next to each other. Write a message across the paper.

3. Unwind the strip and cut the tape. Your decoder will wrap the strip around a pencil to read your message.

Code snake

This clever device can be squashed up so that it fits into a code kit. It's ideal for coding and decoding symbol code messages (page 5).

You will need: strips of red and blue paper, both 1.5cm (¾in) wide and 45cm (18in) long; 52 small self-adhesive dots; tape; pens.

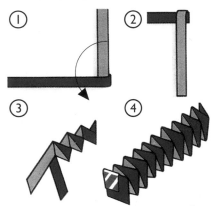

2. Fold the blue strip over the red one. Continue folding the strips over each other until you reach the end. Add tape.

Pull the snake toward you.

When you run out of blue panels, turn the snake over.

4. Stretch the snake to open out the sections. Press 'A' on the first blue panel, then the rest of the letters, in order.

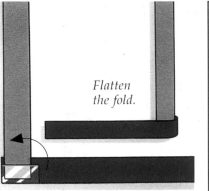

Flatten the fold.

1. Lay the strips as shown in the picture above. Tape the ends firmly together. Fold the red strip over the blue strip.

3. On the dots, write the alphabet with a black pen. With a red pen, draw a code symbol for each letter .

You could use the symbols given for the letter swap code on pages 4-5.

5. On the red panel facing 'A', press a symbol. Then fill all the red panels facing letters with symbols.

A keyword reminder

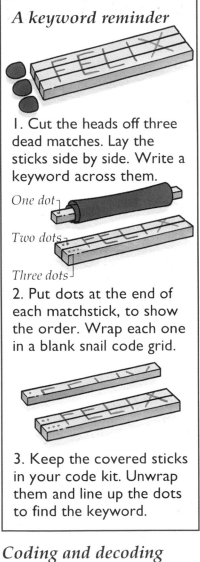

1. Cut the heads off three dead matches. Lay the sticks side by side. Write a keyword across them.

One dot
Two dots
Three dots

2. Put dots at the end of each matchstick, to show the order. Wrap each one in a blank snail code grid.

3. Keep the covered sticks in your code kit. Unwrap them and line up the dots to find the keyword.

Coding and decoding

Stretch out the snake so you can see the letters and symbols clearly.

To code a message, swap each letter for the symbol facing it. To decode, note down the letter facing each symbol.

29

Code games

Treasure trail

This is an ideal party game to play with your friends. The object of the game is to find a treasure which you have hidden. Players can do this by decoding a number of messages which you have hidden at various places along the trail. Make sure that all of the players are familiar with the codes that you have used. To set up a trail, follow the instructions below.

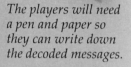

The players will need a pen and paper so they can write down the decoded messages.

Draw yourself a map as a reminder of all the hiding places.

Preparing a trail

Hide the treasure somewhere difficult to find. Each player uses a different set of clues that lead to the same treasure. The last clue in each set says where the treasure is. The first person to find the hidden treasure wins the game.

Give the players any equipment they might need in a code kit (see pages 28-29).

Write the clues before the party, as it may take some time.

1. Write a set of clues in code for each player. Each clue tells the players where to find the next clue.

2. Add symbols (see page 26) to tell the players which keywords and codes have been used.

3. Hide the clues carefully around the house. Give each player their first clue and their code kit.

Treasure map

Decode the clues on this map to discover where the treasure is hidden. There are two sets of clues so you can play with a friend.

Player 1
ALM, ALM

Start here

**ᒧᒥᑕᐺᒧᒣ
ᒣᑕᐺᒧᒣ**

Player 2

You can check your answers on page 32.

Secret teamwork

Baffle your friends by picking out an object which they have chosen in secret. You need an accomplice to line up some objects while you are out of the room. The audience chooses an object. Your accomplice tells you which is the chosen object by the position of your name in the words he uses to call you back. If he says, 'We are ready, Mary', your name is the fourth word, so the object must be fourth in line.

Always count from the left-hand side of the line to find the object.

Mary, you can come in now.

We are ready now, Mary.

Your name is the first word so you know that the chosen object is at the beginning of the line.

The word 'Mary' is the fifth word. This means that the chosen object is in fifth position.

Answers

Letter swap code
page 4
1. Headquarters: Follow Agent X. He may be going far. Take your passport. (a=i)
page 5
1. Agent X: The last forgery is ready. Meet me on the boat. (Keyword: New York)
2. Contact: Soon we will be very rich.

Pigpen code (pages 6-7)
1. This is a good forgery, isn't it?
2. The professor is locked in the tomb. (Keyword: Sophia)

Snail code (page 9)
Brilliant young archeologists find undiscovered tomb filled with jewels. (Keyword: Sphinx)

Calendar code (pages 10-11)
From left to right:
1. Agent X
2. Real statue to be sold
3. Fake statue to go to tomb
4. Fake jewels

Telephone code (pages 12-13)
1. Agent A: All of the jewels in the tomb are fake.
2. Headquarters: Have you seen the professor?
3. Agent A: Who? I do not.....

Morse code (pages 14-15)
1. Do not speak. The tomb is cursed.
2. I know a secret exit in the corner on your side.

Code wheel (pages 16-17)
Key letter: C
1. The label on the box says 'Zanzibar'.
2. Agent A: Professor is safe. Agent X to Zanzibar.

Technobabble (page 18)
1. Contact: Get on the bus. I will put the money under the seat.
2. Agent X: Too late! I took all the money. It is in my bank.
3. 'Lockarium' means 'prison' in technobabble.

Newspaper code (page 19)
Well done, Agent A.

Nifty number code
(page 20)
1. Sphinx
2. Headdress
3. Beads
4. Mummy

Dot code
page 22
1. New York

page 23
1. Suez
2. Tel Aviv

Double and triple bluffs
(pages 26-27)
Double bluffs:
1. I have discovered that one of my slaves has been stealing from me.
2. I have locked him in a tomb on which I have placed a curse.
3. Anyone who speaks in the tomb shall have bad luck. He cannot speak for the rest of his life.

Triple bluffs:
1. Its end always comes before its start.
2. It helps you to write but it's not a pen. (⦿⊞: Code: pigpen; Keyword: Sophie.)
3. It is full of words but it cannot speak.
Answer: Dictionary

Code games
Treasure trail (page 31)
Player 1. from 'start here':
1. Yum, yum (cake)
2. Keeps you dry (umbrella)
3. It's very comfy (cushion)
4. Fruity treasure (fruit bowl)
Player 2. from 'start here':
1. Flower power (flowers)
2. Warm and snug (sweater)
3. Made for walking (shoe)
4. Fruity treasure (fruit bowl)

First published in 1997 by Usborne Publishing Ltd., Usborne House, 83-85 Saffron Hill, London EC1N 8RT, England.
Copyright © 1997 Usborne Publishing Ltd. The name Usborne and the device ♕ are Trade marks of Usborne Publishing Ltd.
UE. First published in America in August 1997. Printed in Portugal.